FIRST PRESBYTERIAN CHURCH

GUESS WHO TOOK THE BATTERED-UP BIKE.

A Story of Kindness

By Raymond & Dorothy Moore

Illustrated by Julie Downing

THOMAS NELSON PUBLISHERS
Nashville • Camden • New York

FIRST PRESBYTERIAN CHURCH

Published in Nashville, Tennessee, by Thomas Nelson, Inc., and distributed in
Canada by Lawson Falle, Ltd., Cambridge, Ontario.

Printed in the United States of America

ISBN 0-8407-6651-3

I like to ride my bike after school. I can ride "no hands" and backward and very fast. One day I was riding over to Trina and Nika's with my pedals flying. I took the corner so fast I rode right into old Mister Bush's yard.

As always, the old sourpuss was sitting on his porch in his rickety old rocker. "Git offa my grass!" he yelled. "Git off—right now!"

His yelling surprised me, and I headed right for
the flower garden. *Crash!* My front wheel hit the border
of rocks, and I and my bike went sailing. Right into Mister
Bush's flowers!

"Now look what you've done!" Mister Bush yelled as he
marched across the yard. "You've smashed my geraniums!"

He didn't even ask if I was hurt. Instead he picked up my bike and
shoved it onto the sidewalk. He gave me a push, too, as I scrambled
out of the flowers.

The wheel on my bike was bent, and my knee was scraped from a
rock. I limped down the sidewalk, pulling my bike beside me.

The twins, Nika and Trina, were sitting on their porch steps. "What happened?" they called when they saw me coming.

"Old Sourpuss made me crash into his flowers," I explained. "Now my bike is wrecked and my knee hurts."

"Let's get Grandpa Ray. He'll know what to do."

The twins' Grandpa Ray lives in a little house right next door to theirs. First he washed off my knee and bandaged the scrape. Then he examined my bike.

"Needs a new wheel, Allie," Grandpa Ray said. "I'm afraid it's too old to be worth fixing."

I felt like crying. "If Old Sourpuss hadn't yelled at me, I wouldn't have crashed," I said. "It's all his fault!"

Grandpa Ray shook his head. "The old codger hasn't been the same since his wife died. Seems to get grouchier every day."

"Grouchier and meaner," I said. "Can't he try to be nice?"

"Guess he feels too sad and lonely," Grandpa Ray explained. "Maybe we should try to cheer him up?"

"How?" the twins asked. I wasn't sure I wanted to be nice to Old Sourpuss. My bike was wrecked and my knee still hurt.

"Let's just think about it awhile," Grandpa Ray suggested.

I dragged my bike home and stuck it behind the garage for the
garbage collectors.

The next day the twins talked about being nice to old Mister Bush.
Trina wanted to bake him a chocolate cake. Nika wanted to take him a
bunch of wildflowers. I decided I would just say hello if I saw him on
his porch.

I got my chance on Tuesday afternoon. Old Mister Bush was sitting
in his rocker when I walked by. "Hello!" I called real loud. But the old
Sourpuss snorted and turned the other way. I knew he was still mad at
me for wrecking his flowers. Well, I was mad about my bike too!

So I walked right up to the porch. "I'm sorry I crashed into your
flowers!" I yelled. "But you made me wreck my bike!" I guess I
surprised him because he stood up so fast he knocked over his rocker.
One of the arms split when it hit the porch. Boy, did I get out
of there fast!

"Now he'll blame me for busting his old chair," I complained to the twins and Grandpa Ray.

Grandpa Ray rubbed his chin. "Seems like the only thing Jeremiah Bush enjoys these days is rocking in that chair," he said. "Maybe we can fix it up for him."

"Let's keep it a secret," Nika suggested. She loves secrets.

So the next morning, Nika, Trina, and I met across the street from Mister Bush's house. While Trina watched the door, Nika and I snuck up on the porch and took the rocker.

All the rest of the week we worked on that old chair in Grandpa Ray's basement. First Grandpa Ray made a brace for the broken arm and glued the crack so it wouldn't show. Then the twins and I sanded the rocker until it felt smooth. Grandpa Ray showed us how to brush the varnish in one direction so it didn't streak. Finally, the chair was ready. It looked as shiny as my mom's new dining room table.

We couldn't wait to take the rocker back. Before school on Monday, Nika, Trina, and I carried the chair back to Mister Bush's porch.

Nika rang the bell, and then we hid in the bushes across the street. Sure enough, Old Sourpuss came out. He stared at his rocker and scratched his head.

"It's a great surprise!" Nika giggled. "He doesn't know who fixed it!"

The next time I passed his house, old Mister Bush was rocking and smiling. But when he saw me, he gave me a funny look. I didn't care. He had an almost new chair, but my bike was wrecked for good.

Then early one morning I saw Mister Bush when I was taking out the garbage. He was driving his old pickup truck out of the alley behind our house. When I turned around, my bike was gone. What was Mister Bush up to anyway? Had he taken my wrecked bike?

When I told the twins what I'd seen, they laughed. "Everyone knows old Mister Bush is a junk collector," Trina said. "He was just looking for more junk in the alley."

But I wasn't sure. I'd never seen him driving down our alley before. It seemed fishy to me.

On Monday afternoon I saw Mister Bush's truck again. I was walking home from my piano lesson. Mister Bush and his truck were headed north on the old schoolhouse road. I was sure he was up to something, but what? The old schoolhouse had been deserted for years.

I hurried to Trina and Nika's house. "I'd sure like to know what Old Sourpuss is up to," I said.

The twins thought I was crazy. But I talked them into riding out to the old schoolhouse. I borrowed my brother's bike, Trina brought a flashlight, and we all wore sneakers. When we got there, Mister Bush's truck was parked under the trees.

"I told you," I said. "Let's see what he's up to."

We crept around the building, peering in the windows. Suddenly Trina stopped. "Shhhhhh! I hear something!" she whispered.

Nika and I heard it too. *Tap, tap, bang. Tap, tap, bang.*

"It's Mister Bush," I said and moved toward the front door. "Look, the padlock's broken."

The twins followed me inside where the noise was louder. We decided to track it down and hurried along a dark hall until we came to a door.

Nika leaned close to listen. "I'll bet it goes to the cellar," she whispered. "That's where the noise is coming from."

I opened the door and started down, shining the flashlight ahead of me. My heart beat so fast I thought it would jump out of my chest. Trina and Nika followed behind me.

At the bottom of the stairs, I saw light coming from under a door across the cellar. *Tap, tap, bang. Tap, tap, bang.* Mister Bush was behind that door hammering on something! "Come on," I said to the twins.

We crept across the cellar, stepping around boxes, old desks, and broken blackboards. When something soft and fuzzy brushed my hair, I almost screamed. But it was only a cobweb hanging from the ceiling. I hurried to the door and looked through the keyhole.

There was Mister Bush, all right. He was standing at an old work table with his back to the door. And right on top of the table was my bike!

"He's pounding on my bike!" I whispered.

"Let me see!" Trina pushed against me and the door swung open. *Bammm!* The door hit the wall behind it.

Mister Bush spun around. "What? . . . Why Trina, Nika—Allie! What are you doing here?"

I marched right to the table and faced the old sourpuss. "What are *you* doing with my bike? I demanded.

Mister Bush put down his hammer. "Somebody fixed my rocker, so I'm fixing your bike," he said. "I had lots of bike parts in my junk collection."

I took a good look at my bike. Mister Bush had already found another front wheel and put it on. Now he was busy pounding out the dents in the fenders.

"Allie, he's fixing your bike like we fixed his rocker!" Trina said.

Mister Bush slapped his knee. "So you're the mystery chair fixers! Seems we all like to do good deeds."

"And keep secrets." Nika laughed.

"Hey, Mister Bush, you're not an old sourpuss after all," I said. I didn't mean it to sound like it did.

Old Mister Bush's face crumpled like a paper bag. "Old Sourpuss? Is that what you kids call me?"

The twins scuffed their feet and looked at the floor. I rubbed my hand over my bike's back fender.

But Mister Bush just picked up his hammer again. "Guess I've been a sourpuss all right," he admitted. "Guess I'd forgotten about the Golden Rule."

"We learned it in Sunday school," Trina said. "Do unto others . . .

". . . as you would have others do unto you," Nika finished.

Mister Bush tapped out another dent on the fender. "Maybe we should make that a habit," he said.

Suddenly Nika started jumping up and down. "We could start a club," she said. "This old schoolhouse could be our clubhouse."

Mister Bush laughed. "Sounds like a real good idea, Nika. But first I want to finish fixing Allie's bike."

I was all for that. I missed riding my bike after school. I wanted to practice riding with no hands.

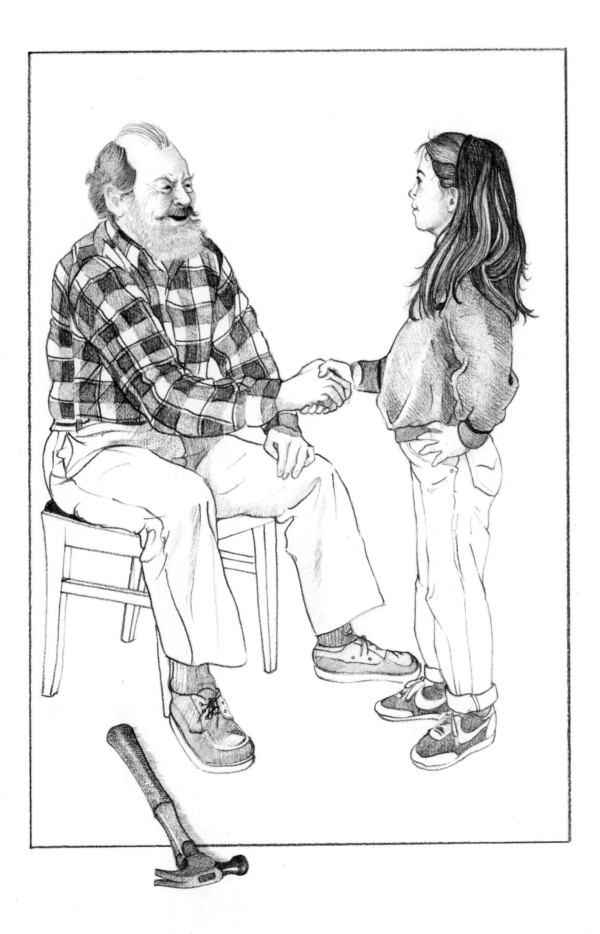

The next Monday Mister Bush delivered my bike in his old pickup truck. I couldn't believe my eyes. The fenders were painted bright blue, my favorite color. The handlebars had new red hand grips. Mister Bush had even fixed the wobble in my bike seat.

I gave Mister Bush a big, quick hug. Then I hopped on my bike and took off for Trina and Nika's house. I just couldn't wait to show the twins and Grandpa Ray my new-old bike.

I know now that nobody is a sourpuss on purpose. People just need to know someone cares. Maybe that's why God thought up the Golden Rule in the first place.

Letter to Parents

Recently Dorothy and I watched as a three-year-old boy beat his baby brother with a teddy bear. Such behavior did not originate in our century. The Moore-McGuffey Readers tell the story of two boys in the early 1800s, who tripped a girl, carrying a bucket of milk, and an old man, just to have fun. In the Bible, irreverent youngsters taunted the Old Testament prophet Elisha, calling him "Old bald head."

Few children are naturally kind. Until the age of three or four, children are not even sociable in a positive sense. Between this age and ten or twelve, they develop adult personalities and, parents hope, a concern for other people.

Your children will seldom be thoughtful unless you explicitly show them how. Base your teachings on the Golden Rule: "Do unto others, as you would have others do unto you" (Matt. 7:12 and Luke 6:31; Lev. 19:18).

Begin with the story in this book. It's natural for kids to think that God just "thought up" the Golden Rule. It's also easy for any of us to ignore rules that have been decided in such a haphazard manner. But God did not just "think up" the rules in the Bible. As our Creator, He knows what will make us happy and healthy. God gave us the Bible as a road map to guide us through life.

The Golden Rule is one of these guides. God knows that we need friends to help us with problems, like the death of someone we love. *Guess Who Took the Battered Up Bike* shows how kids can help other people. End your discussion by asking your children how they might help someone else. If possible, plan at least one activity for your family to do together.

Your next reading of this story could be followed by looking up the Golden Rule in the Bible. God told the Israelites to "love your neighbor as yourself" (see Lev. 19:18).

You might remind your children of the Israelites' miraculous escape from Egypt (see Exod. 14). Now they are camped at the foot of Mount Sinai. Moses is teaching the people how to follow God's ways. Let one of the children read a portion of chapter 19, maybe verses 1 through 3 to set the scene, and then verses 16 through 18.

Jesus expands on the Mosaic version of the Golden Rule in the Sermon on the Mount. Before a child reads these verses, you might describe the outdoor setting of this sermon, the foothills of Galilee. Many other people besides the disciples were sitting on the grass, listening to Jesus.

One child could read Matthew 5, verses 1–12, commonly known as the Beatitudes. Then another child could read verses 43 through 48. Jesus expands upon the Judaic law to include "love your enemies, bless those who curse you."

Finally, have a child read Matthew 7, verse 12, the Golden Rule. This rule is so important that Jesus tells the rich young ruler in Matthew 19 that one must obey the Golden Rule to inherit eternal life. Another day you might read this story in Matthew 19.

The Golden Rule is woven through the well-known religions of our day. And many great men have lived by this rule, like King Arthur, Josiah, Cyrus the Great, and even Nebuchadnezzar in his later years. Share the stories of these great men with your children daily. They will want you to repeat them again and again.

Many of the stories in the Schoolhouse Gang series are adapted from actual experiences. In the early 1960s, Dorothy and I met with several families in Southern California to form such a group. Our children are now mothers and fathers, physicians and nurses, businessmen and homemakers, yet they still talk about the activities we planned. If you introduce elements of surprise and secrecy, children are motivated in remarkably positive ways.

You might wish to join with some friends and form your own club. Our group met every other Saturday night for a potluck supper and meeting. Or your family or a local Boy or Girl Scout group or Awana Club might "adopt" someone in your town. The Golden Rule is an eternal principle, an imprint of the character of God.

Guess Who Took the Battered Up Bike is one of the books in the Schoolhouse Gang series. Other books in the series focus on obedience, honesty, manners, etc. It is our goal to help you share basic Judeo-Christian character values with your children.

Raymond and Dorothy Moore